THE ENCHANTED MANSION

NAVEEN SHARMA

Made with ♥ on the Notion Press Platform
www.notionpress.com

Contents

Preface

The Enchanted Mansion is a tale of mystery, romance, and Gothic intrigue. It is a story that takes place in a secluded mansion, where secrets are hidden in every corner, and ancient curses loom over its inhabitants.

As the story unfolds, readers will follow the journey of Emily, a young woman who is invited to stay at the mansion and quickly finds herself entwined in the lives of its mysterious residents. With the help of a charming and enigmatic man named Alexander, Emily sets out to unravel the mysteries of the mansion and confront the malevolent forces that threaten to destroy everything she holds dear.

This novel is a tribute to the Gothic romance genre, with all its grandeur, opulence, and dark secrets. It is a story that will keep readers on the edge of their seats, with twists and turns that will leave them breathless.

Prologue

"The Enchanted Mansion" is a gothic romance novel that follows the journey of Emily, a young woman who is invited to stay at the mysterious and isolated Enchanted Mansion. As she becomes more entwined in the lives of its inhabitants, she uncovers dark secrets and ancient curses that have plagued the mansion and its surrounding town for generations. With the help of a charming and enigmatic man named Alexander, Emily must unravel the mysteries of the mansion and confront the malevolent forces that threaten to destroy everything she holds dear.

ONE

The Invitation

The story starts with the arrival of an invitation to Emily. As the sun began to set, Emily paced back and forth in her bedroom. She had just received an invitation to stay at the Enchanted Mansion, a grand estate nestled in the heart of the countryside. The invitation was from her distant cousin, Lord Jameson, who she had never met before. Despite feeling hesitant about the invitation, Emily couldn't shake the feeling of intrigue that pulsed through her veins. She had always been drawn to the macabre and mysterious, and the Enchanted Mansion seemed like the perfect place to indulge her fascination.

Emily packed her bags and set off towards the mansion, passing through a dense forest before finally reaching the grand gates. The mansion was even more impressive than she had imagined, with ivy creeping up its stone walls and turrets that reached toward the sky. The butler, a tall, thin man with a stern expression, greeted her at the door and led her into the grand hall.

As Emily looked around, she couldn't help but feel a sense of unease. The mansion was shrouded in darkness, with flickering candles casting eerie shadows on the walls.

But despite the gloom, she couldn't deny the beauty of the place. The walls were adorned with intricate tapestries, and the floors were made of gleaming marble. Emily couldn't help but feel as though she had stepped back in time.

TWO

A Dark and Mysterious Stranger

As the days went by, Emily settled into life at the Enchanted Mansion. She spent her mornings wandering the sprawling gardens and her afternoons reading in the library. But it wasn't until the arrival of a dark and mysterious stranger that her life at the mansion took a dramatic turn.

The stranger's name was Alexander, and he had come to the mansion to oversee the restoration of the estate's crumbling tower. Alexander is a tall and lean man, with chiseled features and piercing blue eyes. He has dark hair that falls in soft waves around his face, and a strong jawline that adds to his overall rugged and handsome appearance. He often dresses in formal attire, which only adds to his air of mystery and sophistication. His demeanor is both charming and enigmatic, making him all the more alluring to those around him. From the moment Emily laid her eyes on him, she felt a strong attraction toward him.

Emily found herself drawn to Alexander, and the two of them soon began spending more and more time together. They would talk for hours, discussing everything from their childhoods to their hopes and dreams. But there was always an underlying tension between them, a sense of longing that neither of them could ignore.

During the conversation, he started explaining the features of the mansion.

He said, "The Enchanted Mansion is an imposing and grand structure, nestled amidst a dense forest on the outskirts of a small town. It is a sprawling estate with towering turrets, intricate stonework, and Gothic architecture that speaks of a bygone era. The mansion is surrounded by a wrought-iron fence, beyond which lies a sprawling garden filled with exotic plants, statues, and fountains. As one enters the mansion, they are greeted by a grand foyer with a high vaulted ceiling and a sweeping staircase that leads to the upper floors. The walls are adorned with intricate tapestries, and there are ornate chandeliers hanging from the ceiling, casting a warm and inviting glow throughout the space.

The drawing room is a particularly opulent space, with plush velvet sofas and armchairs arranged around a large fireplace. There are ornate oil paintings on the walls, and a grand piano stands in one corner, waiting to be played.

The dining room is equally grand, with a long table and high-backed chairs that could easily seat a dozen guests. The walls are lined with intricate wood paneling, and there are elaborate candelabras on the table that cast flickering shadows on the walls.

The bedrooms are spacious and elegant, with canopied beds, silk drapes, and plush carpets underfoot. Each room has its own fireplace, and there are heavy curtains that can be drawn to block out the light."

Despite its grandeur, there is a sense of mystery and foreboding that permeates the mansion. There are hidden passageways, secret rooms, and dark corners that seem to hold untold secrets. The Enchanted Mansion is a place of beauty and danger, of light and shadow, where anything could happen and anyone could be hiding in the shadows."

Now, they both went together to wander in a peaceful environment.

THREE

SECRETS AND BETRAYAL

As the days turned into weeks, Emily began to notice strange occurrences around the mansion. She would hear whispers in the hallways at night, and objects would move of their own accord. She couldn't help but feel as though the mansion was alive, with secrets that were waiting to be uncovered.

It wasn't until Emily stumbled upon a hidden room in the mansion's basement that she realized just how deep those secrets went. The room was filled with strange objects and ancient texts, all pointing towards a dark and sinister past. Emily knew that she had to find out more, but the more she dug, the more dangerous things became.

As Emily delved deeper into the mansion's secrets, she began to realize that nothing was as it seemed. Betrayals and lies lurked around every corner, and she didn't know who she could trust. But through it all, she had Alexander by her side, and together they vowed to uncover the truth about the Enchanted Mansion, no matter the cost.

FOUR

Strange Elements

As Emily and Alexander dug deeper into the mansion's secrets, they uncovered a plot that went far beyond anything they could have imagined. Lord Jameson, Emily's distant cousin, had been using the mansion's dark powers to control the town and its inhabitants. He was willing to do whatever it took to keep his power.

Emily couldn't shake the feeling that there was something strange going on in the Enchanted Mansion. There were too many unexplained occurrences, too many oddities that couldn't be explained away.

Emily thought in her mind,"Despite its grandeur, there is a sense of mystery and foreboding that permeates the mansion. There are hidden passageways, secret rooms, and dark corners that seem to hold untold secrets. The Enchanted Mansion is a place of beauty and danger, of light and shadow, where anything could happen and anyone could be hiding in the shadows."

One day, while wandering the halls of the mansion, Emily stumbled upon a hidden room. It was tucked away behind a bookshelf, and she never would have found it if she hadn't been exploring. Inside, she found an ancient book with strange symbols etched into its cover.

FIVE

SECRETS UNVEILED

As Emily began to read through the book, she realized that it contained secrets that had been kept hidden for generations. It spoke of a curse that had befallen the Enchanted Mansion and the surrounding town, a curse that had caused countless misfortunes and tragedies over the years.

Emily knew that she had stumbled upon something important, something that could change the course of history for the Enchanted Mansion and its inhabitants. But she needed help if she was going to unravel the secrets contained within the book.

She turned to Alexander, knowing that he was the only person she could trust. Together, they pored over the ancient text, deciphering the cryptic symbols and piecing together the clues that would lead them to the truth.

As they delved deeper into the book, they began to uncover a dark history of betrayal, revenge, and unspeakable evil. They discovered that the curse had been cast by a powerful sorcerer named Lord Jameson, who had once lived in the Enchanted Mansion and sought to control the town and all its inhabitants.

With the help of the book, Emily and Alexander uncovered the truth about Lord Jameson's true intentions. He sought to use the curse to maintain his control over the town, and he was willing to do whatever it took to keep his hold on the people.

As they read on, Emily and Alexander knew that they had to act fast. Lord Jameson was a powerful and dangerous adversary, but they were determined to break the curse and put an end to his reign of terror once and for all.

SIX

The Final Confrontation

Emily and Alexander knew that they had to put an end to Lord Jameson's nefarious plans, no matter how dangerous it would be. They spent countless hours poring over the ancient texts in the hidden room, searching for a way to break the curse that had held the mansion in its grip for so many years.

Finally, they found the answer they were looking for. It involved a complex ritual that required the sacrifice of something dear to them both, but they knew that it was the only way to stop Lord Jameson's hold on the town.

They set about preparing for the ritual, gathering the necessary ingredients and carefully laying out the intricate pattern that was required. The night of the ritual was dark and stormy, with thunder rolling in the distance and lightning flashing across the sky.

As they began the ritual, Emily and Alexander felt a powerful surge of energy coursing through their bodies. They knew that they had to stay focused, no matter what distractions came their way. And there were plenty of distractions - Lord Jameson and his minions were doing everything in their power to disrupt the ritual and keep their hold on the town.

But Emily and Alexander refused to be swayed. They pushed forward, their love and determination fueling them as they performed the final steps of the ritual. And then, with a final burst of energy, they broke the curse that had held the mansion in its grip for so long.

SEVEN

TRANSFORMATION OF MANSION

With the curse broken, the Enchanted Mansion was transformed. The darkness and gloom that had once pervaded its halls were replaced with light and life. The gardens bloomed with new vitality, and the mansion's residents were free from Lord Jameson's tyrannical rule.

For Emily and Alexander, the journey had been a long and difficult one. They had faced countless challenges, but through it all, they had come to rely on each other in a way that they never thought possible. And now, as they looked out over the transformed mansion, they knew that they had found something special - a love that was worth fighting for.

As they walked hand in hand through the gardens, Emily couldn't help but feel grateful for the invitation that had brought her to the Enchanted Mansion. Without it, she never would have met Alexander or uncovered the secrets that lay hidden within its walls. And although there would be challenges ahead, she knew that as long as they were together, they could face anything that came their way.

The Enchanted Mansion had been transformed, and so had Emily's life. And as she looked into Alexander's eyes, she knew that she was exactly where she was meant to be.

Conclusion

In the end, Emily and Alexander's quest to break the curse and uncover the secrets of the Enchanted Mansion was successful. They were able to confront Lord Jameson, break the curse, and restore peace to the town and its inhabitants.

Through their journey, they learned that there is often more to people than meets the eye. Everyone has their own secrets, their own fears, and their own inner demons to confront. But it is in facing these challenges head-on that we can truly grow and find our strength.

The Enchanted Mansion taught Emily and Alexander that it is important to be brave, to trust in oneself and others, and to never give up in the face of adversity. It also taught them the value of love, compassion, and forgiveness, and how these qualities can be used to overcome even the darkest of forces.

In the end, the Enchanted Mansion was no longer a place of mystery and danger, but a symbol of hope and perseverance. Emily and Alexander left it behind, knowing that they had not only saved themselves, but also the people of the town who had been living under the shadow of the curse for far too long.

The moral of this story is that no matter how daunting the challenge, we can always find a way to overcome it if we have the courage to face it head-on. We must never give up hope, and always believe in ourselves and in the power of love and compassion to conquer even the darkest of forces.

Printed by Libri Plureos GmbH in Hamburg, Germany